PICTURE BOOK STUDIO

Hans Christian Andersen
translated by Anthea Bell

THE PRINCESS AND THE PEA

illustrated by Eve Tharlet

Once upon a time there was a prince who wanted to marry a princess, but she had to be a real princess. So he went all around the world looking for one, but there was something the matter everywhere. He met plenty of princesses, but he couldn't be sure whether they were real princesses. There was always something not quite right about them.

So he came home again, feeling very sad,
because he did so want to marry a real princess.

One evening there was a terrible storm,
with thunder and lightning,
and the rain poured down.
It was really dreadful!

Someone came knocking at the great gate,
and the old king went to open it.

There was a princess standing outside,
but oh dear, she was in such a state,
what with the rain and the terrible storm!
Water was dripping from her hair and
her clothes, running in at the toes
of her shoes and out at the heels again.
But she said she was a real princess.

Well, thought the old queen, we'll soon see about that!
However, she said nothing, but went into the bedroom,
took all the bedclothes off and put a pea on the bedstead.

Then she took twenty mattresses
and put them on top of the pea, and
after that she put twenty eiderdown
quilts on top of the mattresses.
That was where the princess was to
spend the night.

In the morning, she was asked how
she had slept.
"Oh, very badly!" said the princess.
"I could hardly sleep a wink all night!
Goodness knows what was in my bed!
I was lying on something so hard that
I'm black and blue all over.
It's really terrible!"

So then they could tell she was a real princess,
because she had felt the pea through all twenty
mattresses and twenty eiderdown quilts.
Only a real princess could be as sensitive as that.

Then the prince married her,
for now he knew he had found a real princess,
and the pea was put in a museum,
where it can be seen to this day if nobody
has taken it .

There, that was a real story!

A Michael Neugebauer Book
Copyright © 1987 Neugebauer Press, Salzburg, Austria.
Published and distributed in USA by Picture Book Studio Ltd, Natick, MA.
Distributed in Canada by Vanwell Publishing, St. Catharines.
Published in U.K. by Picture Book Studio, Neugebauer Press Ltd, London.
Distributed in U.K. by Ragged Bears, Andover.
Distributed in Australia by Era Publications, Adelaide.
All rights reserved.
Printed in Italy by Grafiche AZ, Verona.

LIBRARY OF CONGRESS CATALOGING IN PUBLICATION DATA

Andersen, H. C. (Hans Christian), 1805-1875
The princess and the pea.

Translation of: Prindsessen paa aerten.
Summary: By feeling a pea through twenty mattresses and twenty featherbeds,
a girl proves she is a real princess.
1. Fairy tales. I. Tharlet, Eve, ill. II. Title.
PZ8.A542Pq   1987   [E]   87-13913
ISBN 0-88708-052-9

Ask your bookseller for this other PICTURE BOOK STUDIO book
illustrated by Eve Tharlet:
DIZZY FROM FOOLS by M. L. Miller
And these others by Hans Christian Andersen:
THUMBELINE illustrated by Lisbeth Zwerger
THE SWINEHERD illustrated by Lisbeth Zwerger
THE NIGHTINGALE illustrated by Lisbeth Zwerger
THE RED SHOES illustrated by Chihiro Iwasaki
THE LITTLE MERMAID illustrated by Chihiro Iwasaki